Melissa & Alfonso's
FIRST
FAREWELL

Mark Gabriele

Illustrated by Mark Jones

MIRAMBEL

Special thanks to Matt and Becky for bringing Melissa into the world.

Copyright 2012, Mirambel Publishing Company, LLC

ISBN 978-0-9856082-1-7

Library of Congress Control Number: 2012912685

Mirambel Publishing Company, LLC
PO Box 44
South Wellfleet, Massachusetts 02663
www.mirambelpublishing.com

Book and cover design by Kim Shkapich

My name is Melissa. I am the girl in this story.

I have decided to dedicate my book to help kids with disabilities. Many are fine athletes and I love when they get out to show it. The only way to discover what we can do is to step out of our comfort zone and try something new. We're all the same that way.

Melissa, age 14

Following Melissa's wishes, author's royalties from this book will be donated to an organization that benefits kids with disabilities.

M.G.

Of all Melissa's toys, there was one that Melissa loved best. It was a great big purple teddy bear named Alfonso. Alfonso was much more than just a toy to Melissa. Alfonso was Melissa's best friend.

Melissa and Alfonso did **everything** together.
They read books together, had snacks together,

and when they got sleepy, they took their naps together.

One morning at breakfast, Melissa's parents had a surprise.

"Melissa, we're going to go on vacation soon! That means all our time will be just for fun. No work!" said her mother.

"No work, just fun?" Melissa asked, "That sounds great!"

"That's right," continued her mother. "Even for us grown ups! We'll go to a farm, and an aquarium, and to a fun park!"

"We'll even go on a big airplane, and fly up into the clouds!" added her father.

"You mean like the ones I see in the sky?" Melissa asked. Melissa had never been on an airplane before.

"Yes," answered her father. "It will be so much fun!"

It sure sounded good to Melissa. She couldn't believe there was ever a time that grown-ups didn't have to work.

"What about Alfonso?" Melissa asked. "Will he like it too?"

"I don't know," Melissa's mother said, "Do you want to bring Alfonso?"

"Yes, Mommy! Of course!" Melissa replied.

"Well, Alfonso is pretty big. I guess we can call the airline to ask," offered her father.

"Call them, Daddy, call them!" urged Melissa.

Melissa's father called and spent a long time talking to them.
He didn't look very happy. Then he hung up.

"Well, Melissa," he said with very sad eyes, "it seems there's no room on the plane for Alfonso."

"Daddy, are you sure?" she asked.

Her father dropped his head. "Oh, honey – I wish Alfonso could come, but they said the plane is full. Yes, I'm sure."

"I don't think I want to go anymore, Mommy," Melissa said, with a big tear rolling down her cheek.

"It will just be for a week, Melissa. I'm sure Alfonso will wait for you. You'll see him again when we come back home."

"A whole week without Alfonso?" she exclaimed. That seemed like forever. "Oh, no!" she cried. Then she grabbed him and ran into her room.

After she closed the door, she flopped down on her bed and said, "Oh, Alfonso, what are we going to do?"

"Don't worry, Melissa," Alfonso said. "You go ahead. I can stay here and play with your toys."

"But Alfonso, don't you want to come with me?"

"Of course I do, Melissa! But I don't want you to give up your trip if I can't go. I will just see you when you get back. You'll have so much fun, Melissa. Why don't you go?" said Alfonso.

Melissa took a deep breath. Finally she spoke. "Okay Alfonso, I'll go."

On the day they were going to leave, Melissa was mostly quiet all morning. When it was time to pack, Alfonso helped her pack her suitcase. He was quiet too. It was almost time to say goodbye.

"I'm ready to go, Alfonso," Melissa said sadly.

She took her hair ribbon out of her hair and gave it to him. "Here, Alfonso. Will you hold this for me until I get back?"

"Yes, Melissa. I'll take very good care of it."

With a tear in her eye, Melissa said "Goodbye, Alfonso."

"Goodbye, Melissa," Alfonso said, "I'll miss you!"

"I'll miss you too," said Melissa.

This was the first time they ever had to say goodbye to each other, and it made them both very sad. Then they hugged and hugged and hugged.

"Come on, let's go!" called Melissa's father. They got into their car and were off!

"Where's your favorite ribbon, Melissa?" asked her mother in the car.

"Alfonso is keeping it for me until we get back," Melissa replied.

After Melissa left, Alfonso went over to Melissa's

toys and picked one out to play with.

On the first day of vacation, Melissa's parents took her to a farm. She saw all kinds of animals she had never seen before. It was time to feed the lambs. The farmer let Melissa give them some bread.

Back home, Alfonso went for a walk in the woods. He saw all kinds of animals he had never seen before. He saw some rabbits that were looking for food. Alfonso gave them some bread.

The next day Melissa's parents took her to the aquarium to see all the different kinds of fish. Melissa saw three big goldfish.

Back home, Alfonso passed the pond and looked into the water. Alfonso saw three big goldfish.

The day after that, Melissa's parents took her to the fun park. Melissa went on the roller-coaster ride and zoomed down the tracks.

Back home, Alfonso pushed his wagon to the top of a big hill.
He climbed in and zoomed down the hill.

But even though Melissa was having fun, she thought about Alfonso all the time.

And even though Alfonso was having fun too, he missed Melissa very much.

"I hope Melissa is coming home today," he said. And he said it every day.

Finally, it really was the day!! Melissa was coming home!
She packed up her suitcase, got on the plane, and was on
her way back.

Alfonso was playing outside when he saw a car coming up
the street. He watched it and watched it. Sure enough, it
was Melissa's car. That meant Melissa must be inside!

"Melissa, is that you?" Alfonso called out.

"Yes, Alfonso, it's me. I'm home!" said Melissa. She was so happy to see him again that she ran over to give him a big hug.

"Would you like to hear about my trip?" Melissa asked.

"I sure do!" said Alfonso, "and I want to tell you about all the things I did!"

They told each other their stories. They were amazed to find out they had done so many similar things.

Most of all they were just happy to be back together again. They played and played, and talked and talked, until it got to be night time.

When they both got tired, they fell asleep, just like they had always done before.

The End

A Note from the Author

Children care deeply about the world around them. Unfortunately, the background noise of a commercial culture can easily drown this out.

Many years ago I began writing books for children I know, making them the central character of the story. I gave each the hand-illustrated original. Publishing them now is an extension of that gift—my author's royalties will be dedicated to whatever charitable cause they choose. I invited each child to designate a purpose for their book, and to write the book's dedication where they could explain their choice. They were all happy to be asked, and these books remain very much theirs. Then, prepared with a short list of questions to discover where their empathies lay, I sat with each child in quest of the dedication.

Each book in this series will support an organization whose mission matches what matters most to each child. It is my hope these books will serve as living instruments of each child's intention, through which they can see the impact on the world that their caring can make.

— Mark Gabriele

Other books from Mirambel Publishing

J.D.'s Scratch Match
Sofia's Backwards Day
Elena's Big Cheese Squeeze
Detective Dante

www.mirambelpublishing.com

Made in the USA
Charleston, SC
14 September 2012